KNIGHTHOOD & ITS CHALLENGES:
THE ORDER OF EXCALIBUR

KNIGHTHOOD & ITS CHALLENGES:
THE ORDER OF EXCALIBUR

VASILIOS D'MILLION

Archway Publishing books may be ordered through booksellers or by contacting:

Archway Publishing
1663 Liberty Drive
Bloomington, IN 47403
www.archwaypublishing.com
844-669-3957

Use logo for Scripture and Science, Inc.

ISBN: 978-1-6657-5171-1 (sc)
ISBN: 978-1-6657-5172-8 (e)

Library of Congress Control Number: 2023919663

Print information available on the last page.

Archway Publishing rev. date: 10/12/2023

DISCLAIMER

All characters depicted in this fictional Medieval Chivalric romance and the affects of early Christianity derive from the imagination of the author, and, therefore, do not reflect the identity of any person alive or dead. Any character resemblances to a person alive or dead are purely coincidental, and in no way are designed to be disrespectful or leave any stain of ill-repute towards them.

Scripture and Science, Inc.

"...where faith & rationale agree..."

Since 2019

My praise to the Lord Jesus Christ
for directing my way to both establishing this nonprofit
and persuading me to write this novella about serving the Lord,
Knights, Chivalry, and those who thirst for Him and redemption

CONTENTS

PREFACE

My account of the fictional medieval life of a Knight is the basis for my imaginative impression of historical events I've experienced, seen, read, or studied over my few years on this planet.

Years ago, I followed the path of my nation that encouraged kids to get a good education in order to get a good job. But one day I found myself overqualified for any decent-paying job. Was it my fault I earned a BA in English, an MS in community counseling, a PsyD in Clinical Psychology, and an EdS in e-Learning?

I'm still a Christian, a dreamer, a geek, an ordained minister, a postsecondary psychology professor, a US Air Force disabled veteran, and a retiree, wonderfully married, and senior citizen of America. I have always favored stories with a science-fiction or science-fact background, along with being attracted to adventure, sword and sorcery, and revelations from the Bible. I might be called a kind of a Renaissance person, overlaid with science rationale and grounded in theology.

The nonprofit company Scripture and Science Inc. will use this novella as a stepping stone towards bringing Holy Scripture and science under the same banner of God's fulfillment for humankind's better knowledge of the universe they struggle to define. The Order of Excalibur will serve as a starting point within my church—Disciples of Christ Fellowship—for personal and community maturity. Starting in early grade school, at an age of eight or nine, children, and later teens and adults, will become Knights through a gradual program of spiritual, psychological, and physical growth and development to foster courtesy and compassion. Completing this program will allow girls and women to use the title Dame with their given name, and boys and men Sir.

I close by expressing my undying devotion to the love of my life, my spouse and my sister in Christ, Lillian, for making my life livable.

PROLOGUE

The rain had eased into a misty sprinkling on the fur of the rider's coat after the former downpour. Ealdhelm Benedict von Hohensee, the current Duke of Cnobheresburg, strode confidently toward the pub. He often performed this silent inspection of nearby towns and villages—unawares by them—to gauge their loyalty to himself and their general well-being, and their service to his East Anglia Dukedom.

I'll have to keep track of my activities some how. History happens, I understand, while events are actually happening more than what's to take place.

I'm also trusting that my light suit of mail, with my single-edged knife—a Seax--8 and 31 cm (3 and 12 in)—at my side, doesn't give me away. I've wearing a dark-coloured, hooded cloak to further disguise myself. I like to find out first hand what my people think of me, especially, in these trying times. I want to depend upon them in battle, not for giving me respect in a drinking hall.

He looked over his shoulder in time to watch a bright rainbow arching across the land. *Before long, sunset would signal the close of another busy day. Maybe the Lord has a few surprises in store for me yet.*

Standing at his full six-foot stature, carrying his 240-pound body weight a little better these days, he went inside and scanned the crowd habitually for any signs of trouble or remembered vendettas if he was recognized. The Duke tethered his warhorse in the adjacent stable, well inside its coverings so as not to give away that a high royal person was in the immediate area.

Noting no threat of attackers, he slowly eased his fair-complexioned face inside.

I'll take this corner table-and-bench, with my back to the wall, so I'll have a good view of things. I'll slide my Seax to my left side so if there's a problem, no one will see my blade until it drinks deep of their bodily juices.

"Hail, yir Lawdship," the innkeeper earnestly shouted. "The usual, m'lawd?" he asked expectantly.

I was getting used to not having his Storm-Bringer within easy reach (i.e., is thirty-seven-inch, double-edged Tang sweord), or his plumed helmet of purple-n-gray, shield, or lance. But I reminded myself that this was not my castle, but these were some of my soldiers.

While preparing to answer the inn-keeper, a scuffle broke out a few tables to the visitor's right. The Duke casually kept a watchful eye on it.

In days gone by, this scene would never have occurred, when he and his family ruled this area without question. My warriors conducted themselves with good graces. But how things have changed since then ... a lot, in fact.

"My dear inn-keeper, let's keep it...ya know...quiet...where my person is concerned, alright? And here's some extra coins for ya. And bring a tankard of ale and some cheese with a bread slice," the Duke ended, hoping to continue his stealthy presence among his town's people.

My beloved Duchess. How I'm trying to fulfill my husbandly and monarchy duties to maintain the highest standards as a Knight wearing an Excalibur ring. The Code of Conduct guides my affairs with the community and persons under my charge, as well continually to adhere to the same principles of Knighthood as the mythical King Arthur of Medieval literature dictated.

My striving to maintain my Order of Excalibur push among my knights-n-training and beyond is to make the tales of Arthur more believable. An actual ring—turquoise stone with small silver sweord—is worn on the Chevalier aspirant's second finger to the right of the eventual wedding band finger is symbolic of their commitment as a Squire, then onto Knighthood, in better relating to our Chivalric Code obligations. For them, that ring will be like having a piece of Excalibur as their guiding inner light to successfully embody the Code of Conduct and Chivalric Code that's always with them.

I'm striving to maintain my devotion to the Order, which means faithfully adhering to Jesus and His church teachings, defending the weak and helpless, treating girls and women with respect.

With my refreshments in hand, I wished I could tell my beauteous Duchess of Cnobheresburg—Gwenllian, all aglow with her red hair cascading towards her feet, her emerald eyes adding to a sheen of blondness about her hair and complexion, even more fair than his, and a warming and welcoming smile—that the stress of war was nearing its end. But alas, it's not to be so.

He sat back on his bench to enjoy this repartee while pondering unspoken thoughts. *I wonder what marvels of warfare I could entertain to help my men-at-war get through the repeated attacks by those Danes and soon...the warriors of Mercia ...? Not that we haven't held our own, but...I want to keep a head of the battle before it happens to insure my people the victory...*

Suddenly, the Duke's warmer thoughts were rudely interrupted by an unannounced visitor. A drunken form stumbles his way over to the Duke's table-n-bench set-up, shaking the Duke out of his revelry about his wife and Excalibur issues. But sensing no danger, he used his right-booted leg to roughly push the merrymaker aside to land on someone else's refreshments.

When the innkeeper rushed over offering a thousand pardons for the drunk's intrusion, I held my fingers to my lips for quiet so as not to alert the room. Amid the sudden action on my part, the inn drew still. I gave the innkeeper some extra coins to cover the spilt refreshments on that other group's benches, and to replenish my order as well.

"See to it," I told him so as to refocus the attention of onlookers on their carousing, and not some cloathed stranger.

The Duke tried to play it under cover so as not to stimulate wagging tongues for hire. *I'm always aware of how folks may talk big about what they think they know, yet don't have a clue. Then there's any number of other details about his kingdom that loose lips or attracting clothing would loudly proclaim.*

Slowly, the rough jollity resumed as everyone came to realize that they would not be spending time in the Duke's castle awaiting certain death for disturbing someone, possibly a Lord. They hadn't known who the stranger was, except that he was probably rich enough to pay for their refreshments. They were farmers, animal herders, craftsmen, and fishermen, but when called to, they'd suit up and join their Duke's cadre of warriors. But now, it was time to consume another round of drinks and air more stories about their daring do on real and imagined battles.

Later on that evening, the Duke disappeared through a side door hidden by a dark curtain, hardly noticed by the even drunker patrons. *Let them have their spoil while they can, for in a few days hence … well…it will not be so merry.*

The Duke could not understand how things had changed so much since the early days of settlements in what has come to be known as the East Anglia part of England. *I'm making history, I suppose, withstanding these standoffs against the Mercians and the Danes. It's very much like the tale of King Arthur and his Round Table of Knights who followed the Order of Excalibur to bring integrity and compassion in following the Lord Jesus. Arthur's sword, Excalibur, was as much magical from the "Lady of the Lake" as it was victorious on the battlefield. Ever symbolic as Excalibur, the rings I had forged favor that kind of connection with that romance tale to highlight my Knight's prestige and wholesomeness.*

But we did not have to contend with that evil Morgana and her co-conspirators in the fiction of Arthur's Knights, where we are dealing with those Mercians and Danes.

My, how the evening turns chilly nowadays after spending a few drinking and eating hours with my townspeople. When I get to the castle, I'll be extra cautious about my goings-on, especially when it comes to preparing for another round of would-be conquerors against those blood-thirsty Vikings and Mercians.

Chapter One

LOOK-BACK

The Duke of Cnobheresburg had a loving family, a loyal horde of Knights, archers, pikemen, shield-bearers, and footmen who vowed to hold their own against any would-be conquerors, especially the Mercians or the Danish Vikings. He had concerns about his accomplishments up to this time, considering the upcoming battle with those Mercians, and what legacy he's to leave behind for his son the Marquis, his daughter Lady Diot, his youngest Lady Kiaborough, and most importantly, for his bride of many decades, his Duchess.

When I was growing up, eventually entering my own Knighthood training as a Page, my father told me this tale. He told me about Roman rule up to the fifth century in the Year of our Lord. He mentioned that several different groups sacked the eternal city, starting in the Year of Our Lord 390. The darkness represented the absence of Roman rule after nearly six centuries of its influence. Viking raids, hordes of fellow Teutonic German Jutes, Angles, Saxons, and Frisians were setting up their permanent territory, and the resultant battles for land and resources made it almost impossible for peace to settle in East Anglia.

Being a Knight became one of my answers to rebuilding this post-Roman world into a new and hopefully better land where people can raise a family, earn a living, and feel protected by a strong and well-trained militia. This way of life can be hard at times, but with our Lord Jesus' guidance, and my Knighthood experiences, it seemed to be the next best thing to having a similar aura of civilization like Rome had been.

My involvement in Knighthood would overshadow my future Code of Conduct aspirations that compel me to live as a Knight to live up to a moral and ethical way of life with Jesus as my Lord. I knew it also let me know of my duty and compassion for women, girls, and elders—much like an Order of Excalibur member. For me, the life of King Arthur and his Round Table of Knights pointed the way for me to rise above the violence and sheer lack of courtesy and responsibility that so characterized this new age of living. I offered that Excalibur ring to Squires as their connection with real the Chivalric Code and the Arthurian legend.

The Duke briefly described the key tenants of this Code of Conduct for Knighthood from his own experiences.

When I was a Page, three major principles were drilled into me: a will to obey God, a will to work by God's design, and marriage. That third principle involves coming to know the relationship between Jesus and His church, the Ecclesia. Jesus' church is His bride. As a man, you live well when you take care of yourself because you love that God made, formed, and created all people. The marriage between a man and a woman is God's salute to His greatest creation, humankind, in allowing that couple to experience agape—God's love—on a very human level.

The Duke wanted to point out, too, that his father also had a lot to do with his aspirations to Knighthood and of being the best leader his domain would ask of him.

Thus, my father said, loving Jesus as a Knight allows the aspirant to experience the love of God through a Knight's expression of his personality, being brave, courteous, loyal, and compassionate. The Order of Excalibur, then, becomes a remembrance of taking that agape love of God and translating it into a visible show of God's will in your life. King Arthur was legendary but a Knight's way under the Order of Excalibur is real.

He later added his knowledge of history as it pertains to his domain and culture. *Charlemagne, or Charles the Great, became the first example of Chivalry among my people, with his Code of Conduct to help keep his Knights under his control by demonstrating their following his rules: devotion to serving our Lord and Savior, duty to their liege lord, and courteous treatment of women, children, and old people.*

My father went on to tell me about the onslaught of these woeful times following the demise of Rome. We're having our struggles with the persistent challenge of the Danes along our Angles' North Sea holdings.

Trouble also came from the ruling Heptarchy—a Greek term—for seven kingdoms formerly sharing power. They included East Anglia, Essex, Kent, Mercia,

Northumbria, Sussex, and Wessex. Things eventually fell apart, leaving the Mercians in the Year of Our Lord 794 demanding to rule their lesser, former Heptarchy members, including East Anglia.

I understood my recall of history at the knee of my father. He was right in the middle of imminent change and practically on the cusp of greater change, like me, his son...and my son...who will one day...take over...from me...

Chapter Two

GATHERING

In early March of the Year of Our Lord 805, I put out a call to arms to rally my troops for battle by the side of their Duke of Cnobheresburg. All my troops should be here over the next fortnight. I only know my battle plans.

The Duke didn't say what his battle plans were as he continued to reveal some of his war chest of notions. He just wanted them there as a show of force to his enemies, who would be eager to stir up what they may toward his force's undoing. The Duke never took kindly to traitors or liars in his midst.

Let them do their worst, from which I hope to greatly benefit. But, ho, something's amiss at the drawbridge.

"Guard, what have ye?" the Duke called down to the gatekeeper from one of the castle's windows overlooking the fortified frontage and watchtower where a small entourage of horsemen had stopped their mounts.

In response, the smiling face of his son, the Marquis Aldus Benedict von Hohensee, came into view, with his hefty length of golden hair falling all around his head, and a thick beard. His gray eyes betrayed the even temper he tried to affect—sometimes flashing greenish-brown or even purple, if he was that irritated by something or someone. His happy countenance befitted his high respect and trust in his father's call to arms and leadership in East Anglia. He had just returned from a patrol of their East Anglia borders.

The Marquis was above average in height—six foot two—weighing a little under 220 pounds. He carried his Saxon war helmet under his left arm as was custom for warriors welcomed to their castle, or when visiting another Lord's keep. He was dressed in a similar livery as his father. The Marquis was ready for battle with his *sweord*, the same make as his father's, named Lightning. He also had a troop of Knights as his escort.

"What news say ye, son of my flesh and blood, and a better Chevalier than me, I'll wager?" The Duke laughed. "Get him settled so we may soon embark upon our plan against the Mercians," the Duke says to his servants nearby.

After my heir apparent joined me and his fellow Chevaliers and other officer warriors, we sat down to some refreshments during my war counsel. The next Mercian incursion was our topic for the day. I've settled upon a war campaign that I hoped would keep the Mercians at bay, but first, he must deal with the more immediate Danish threat.

As an aside to the mounting pressure to be fully prepared for the Danes, the Duke told me, thoughtfully, that he trusts they won't be any further problems until he and his immediate family are safely buried at his beloved chapel near his Burgh Castle. But that kind of thinking would not enable the Lord of this realm to be successful against his mortal enemy, the Mercians. It was only his imagination, after all—a hoped-for, lasting peace, with himself and his family. The Duke understood that the struggles of East Anglia against the Mercians and the Danes would take immense resources, especially men-at-arms. He was mindful of the food, weapons, and health of his victorious horde, who still needed to be resupplied after their last encounter in time for the next onslaught of the invaders.

The Duke did dream of never having to fight again, but alas, the Mercians and the Danes didn't look like they would be eliminated any time soon. That longed-for state of eternal peace made the Duke recall the recent Mass in his chapel, and some comforting thoughts.

Bishop Arian Hardewood and I... were not ...friends. I was always careful not to sound judgmental about my keep's spiritual advisor. He knew the Bishop was his connection with God as the Duke struggled to keep his family and his kingdom safe.

The Duke believed that the Bishop was a good friend in a way that anyone could call a Cleric...a friend. It started back during the reign of his family as Duke of this fief. The younger Duke-to-be didn't seem to be too bright when it came to things of faith, according to the then Parish Priest Hardewood. He would bewail his misgivings about the younger Duke to the elder Duke, with an air of distaste and woe. His father tried talking to his Duke-to-be about such things, but it only served to drive them apart. The young Duke-to-be held the notion that Father Hardewood had it in for him…Hell possibly—because he wasn't a worthwhile student of God's way of life.

From the Priest's viewpoint, now the Bishop, the young Duke-to-be didn't appear to be a good candidate for the East Anglia crown.

Ever since the Bishop entertained his not-so-pleasant notion of the younger Duke-to-be, he made as if to help his young princeling achieve the Cleric's notion of a servant of God and a good soldier, who might just make Knighthood. His Priest made it a point to not only point out the duke-to-be's shortcomings—in grammar, literature, and history, among others—he also doubled up his dislike for the duke-to-be's handling of a wooden sword.

I didn't do well, no matter that I was the region's heir apparent to the East Anglia throne. No matter how many Masses I attended, good deeds around the realm, or improvement in Knighthood training, I never seemed to measure up, according to Bishop Hardewood. But he never did things openly to draw attention to his troubling perceptions of me.

The only way the duke-to-be and then Priest Hardewood got along was for the then Squire for the Dukedom to stay one step ahead of his priest by never failing to do what he was told to do, especially when it came to things of the spirit. Among these seemingly endless arrays of "near-perfections," the duke-to-be managed to satisfy his Priest with such actions as his steadfast prayer mannerisms, his eventual attention to his fencing artistry, and his devotion to his parents.

Father Hardewood seemed to be comfortable with my improved standing on some of my Code of Conduct and my own Order of Excalibur aspirations. If I didn't look like a Knight yet, my continued following of my Priest's counsel would surely make me more like the man—and leader—I'm destined to be. As time went on, we became begrudging partners in our efforts to see me through Knighthood, and eventually, becoming the new Duke.

Bishop Hardewood was his usual self when he stopped by to pray for us and the upcoming Mercian onslaught. He was adorned in his drab priestly vesture of gray and white with the hood resting on his back. He had every appearance of piety. His people should see him when he's not so holy—arguing with me and others--about which he emphasized his notion of living by God's Word, the Bible, apart from the world's attractions, but I quibble here.

I remembered the Bishop talking about the Judgment to come when Jesus will Rapture—raise the dead in Christ, then the living in Christ, to Heaven—those who "do justice, love mercy, and walk humbly with thy God," as written in Micah 6:8.

I have often pondered my life's accomplishments when compared to my Lord's plan for me, I mused. I felt I often had fallen short of His plan for my eternity. I'll try to do better out of the lot I have, particularly for my family and my realm. It's often a hard life.

The bishop is a man of God, to be sure, but sometimes he doesn't seem to envision me as a ruler here. How am I supposed to serve God and serve his Cleric too? I don't need to be pulled in different directions with an upcoming battle to prepare for. But I may at least let our Lord and Savior guide the both of us towards His plan for our future.

It was a brisk, sunny Spring morning, and the wind seemed to give witness to another scene of humankind's art for destruction, albeit a defense of cherished land and resources. *If it wasn't for this upcoming battle to maintain our freedom, there could be folks enjoying a picnic, some kind of play, and definitely not a preparation for war here. It's a great place just to relax. I trust that my war band will be sufficient enough to route the Mercians. Oh ... I'm sorry for trying to wax poetic, I scolded myself.*

The plain rose gently as they came upon the bluff overlooking one of the valleys of Norfolk, several leagues southwest of Burgh Castle, I made note of. The Duke's cohort had the higher ground, affording them a slight advantage as they approached their foe.

"What say ye, my son and captain?" the Duke shouted over the breeze attempting to blow them off the field as another sign of the impending battle's futility.

"Aye, milord. We're up to standard on this—another effort for us to remain free. I trust that you've let my mother the Duchess know that you'll be home in time for supper after this hopefully brief victory is set in stone, eh?" the Marquis laughed." It'll be a victorious March day when we set those Mercians to route," his captain of his host said with humor and confidence.

"I'll take that confidence, and make it our victory toast at our banquet this eve, oh gallant Chevalier of my host," the Duke added with great expectations of his own.

He waited among his warriors, all clad in the House of Hohensee's livery—purple vestments highlighted with gray. The Duke's shield was resplendent with his great bear and a powerful hawk in gold facing inward, jaws grimacing and claws up, and surrounded by the purple and gray adornment of the Duke's Hohensee name. His helmet was also of a typical Saxon gray steel, with a multicolored plumage.

Chapter Three

BATTLE

The Duke's Chevaliers valiantly held their mounts in check. It was a brisk March before dawn in in the year of our Lord 806, with a nearly cloudless blue sky. Almost as one, the Duke's knights raised their Tang sweords out of their scabbards and waved them high about their heads. The Duke also raised the mighty Storm-Bringer, and his son the Marquis his sword Lightning. His archers were scattered among their fellow soldiers as a key offensive stance. Their footmen with pikes and large shields, and the infantry with spears, began stamping their feet while intoning their Duke's family refrain from the "Anthem of the Teutonic Knights":

> *Rise! You will never die, praying to the sky,*
> *Waiting for the answer you'll never deny,*
> *Marching for the brave with one foot in the grave,*
> *Surviving the rest of the night.*

Shortly after the Duke's host's stirring Anglo-Saxon refrain, the dust and howling from the advancing Mercians overwhelmed the battlefield in announcement of their advance. It was like an out-of-control feast that spilled into the dusty roadways, making such a din that peaceful folk would have a hard time getting rest that evening.

As the commander of his host of loyal Knights, footmen, archers, and spearmen, the Duke rode confidently in and around his horde, resplendent in his fief's purple and gray, whipping his people into a fighting frenzy to win the day.

The clash of men at arms came swift, like one of the Duke's predatory falcons spying the terrain below before pouncing upon its prey. The Mercians were well rehearsed in their efforts to undo the Duke's line of action. Dressed in their Saxon helmets with shields on their left arms, with swords, axes, or spears, the Mercians waved their weapons around and in the air while riotously howling their intent to do great bodily harm to their sworn enemies of East Anglia.

The clash of bodies and metal was like a mob of crazies with only one purpose: putting an end to East Anglian sovereignty and including them in their growing conquests. The Duke's forces and their Mercian adversary's line of battle seemed to foster special fighting abilities that could turn the tide of battle this way or that.

The Duke kept his sword arm busy with thrusts, parries, and blocks while keeping his shield in use as his other fighting implement. Mighty Storm-Bringer drank deep of Mercian blood that flowed like an uncorked wine decanter unavoidably knocked out of its cradle. The Duke's swinging motion severed limbs, cut off heads, and nearly split men in half while Storm-Bringer sang her song of death and carnage.

It was, indeed, a horrendous battle. Fighting on horseback is not as simple as the Chevalier's training might lead some people to believe. But the Duke was thankful to the Lord for being Knighted to serve his realm on such occasions as this.

Amid this deadly melee, the Duke's Chevaliers held their own slightly apart from either side's footmen, spearmen, and Knights. His shield men with their overlarge shields maintained their steady rhythm towards the Mercian line, pushing their enemy line with their eight-foot pointed pikes through their solid wall of armor. Behind the shield-bearers were footmen with pikes jabbing and stabbing Mercians through their overlarge shields while continuing their forward motion.

The Duke's chevaliers were a force to be reconned with. His footmen appeared to waver back and forth on the front line, but the Duke felt his horde could hold against them. Later, his forward line appeared to weaken, as if about to shatter altogether. Yet some newfound energy seemed to stimulate the Duke's host to a higher level of warfare not usually displayed. While footmen, spearmen, and pikemen, and shield-bearers surged forward, the Duke's archers laid waste to the Mercian band with a steady flow of arrows well aimed and deadly in their targeting.

The sun was also doing its best to wear down the Duke's horde: arms ached, breathing became labored, their vision was bleary by sweat, and their blood flowed freely from wounds grievous with mortal injuries.

I prayed that what gods there were would deliver them from the onslaught before he and his host lost everything near and dear to them. Then I quickly put my faith where it always was, with my Lord and Savior Jesus Christ. I hastily asked the Lord Jesus for His forgiveness and that he not blame my people for my slip of the tongue.

Shortly thereafter, the Duke of Cnobheresburg returned to his holdings and castle. His horde held fast that day of the battle, but many felt and displayed victory's often twisted anthem of pain and suffering amid the joyful knowledge that they held the day. He attended the Lord in the chapel before seeking redress of his injuries.

The Duke's wounds were serious and not so easy to treat. He would not let his fair duchess visit him in their infirmary until, as he said, he "looked like the Chevalier he was." He wanted to spare her the pain of seeing the man she loved suffering beyond her imagination. Of course, no one can deny the Duchess of the castle her right to be at her beloved's side, especially in his hour of pain and suffering. And so they were again—the Duke and Duchess of Cnobheresburg--comforting each other.

Chapter Four

AFTERMATH

When the Duke strolled into his audience chamber after a few days of rest and re-cuperation, his retinue of Chevaliers and officers of his footmen, archers, pikemen, spearmen, and shield-bearers came to attention with a rousing cheer for their sovereign. "Huzzah! Huzzah!"

The Duke returned their accolade with his own "Huzzah!" and joined them in gulping down Mead[1†] from pewter goblets filled to the rims. The Duke's loveable mastiffs—combined, more than four-hundred pounds with one male, one female, and their puppies—joined in for a hearty evening of fun. They barked periodically while their human masters laughed, ate, and made merry.

"Now let the merrymaking commence, everyone. You've earned it," the Duke encouraged them as they clashed their mugs.

In the meantime, he had ordered the watch doubled so as not to be caught napping during this festive moment even after so grand a victory over the Mercians. He knew that spies and traitors would love to enrich their purses at his kingdom's expense. But he wasn't about to let that happen. He loved his Duchess, his children, and his kingdom. He would never go down without a fight.

I considered this war to be my time of trial to earn the right to be called a Chevalier. It was magical, and very spiritual. The Order of Excalibur was an occasion for spiritual, physical, and psychological maturity, starting about age eight. Ceremony was of utmost importance for young and old, Ladies and Knights, and

---

[1] [†] Mead, an intoxicating liquor, was made from fermenting honey mixed with water and sometimes fruits, spices, grains, or hops. Its potency measured 3.5–18 percent alcohol by volume.

rulers of every stature in the East Anglia realm. It was this attention to word and deed that wedded me into a solemn event for a Page matriculating through becoming an aspiring Squire. That also sustained me through this most recent display of success as a Knight.

Chapter Five
KNIGHTING

There were several pronouncements, according to the Duke of Cnobheresburg, that acknowledged the degree of preparation completed to step into each portion of Knighthood.

Cleansing was the first hurdle as a young Knight-to-be at the age of eighteen. I thoroughly washed for the occasion, as was the custom of persons of this stature, usually once every other month.

Clothing was next with my white vesture, red robe, and black hose and shoes, all symbolizing mortality.

Prayer was the next value while in the chapel, where I contemplated my life, my place in Jesus's plan for me, inclusive of obeying God, doing His will, and properly (i.e., love, compassion, support, loving, honor) loving a woman.

Weapons were of value to a Knight, wherein I laid my sword—to be named Storm-Bringer—my shield, and my spurs upon the altar.

After my solitary vigil in the chapel, my spiritual advisor, then Father Arian Hardewood, conducted the remaining ceremony as an extension of the Mass. I attended the ceremony with my father, the the Duke, and by Father Hardewood and two sponsors for the actual Knighting.

The new Duke's sponsors presented him before the chapel assemblage and to his Liege—his father, the Duke of Cnobheresburg--along with his sword, shield, and spurs, with his family's purple and gray heraldry emblazoned upon his shield. He then he gave his word for his Fount of Honor through his vow and oath as follows.

For his *Adoubement*, also known as the accolade or dubbing, sponsors presented him before the congregation with his tools of Knighthood: the sword Storm-Bringer, spurs, shield, and family heraldry on his vestments.

He then made his *vow*: never traffic with traitors; never give evil counsel to a lady; whether married or not, treat her with respect and defend her against all; observe fasts and abstinences; and every day attend Mass and make an offering in church.

The *Oath* then acknowledged his sincerity, backed up by the threat of divine retribution should his uttering prove false, so as not to have committed a crime against God, which would lead to eternal damnation. The following notations completed the Duke's Knighting.

In the *Dubbing*, his liege then presented him with his sword, buckling it on his belt, then handed him his shield and spurs.

The *Colee* came next. His father said, "I dub thee, Sir Leopold, the Marquis of Cnobheresburg," while tapping the flat of his blade on his left shoulder, then his right shoulder, then left again, "a Chevalier of the realm, henceforth and into eternity," finishing with apparent joy and relief. (The young Marquis' elevation to Duke would take place in a later ceremony.)

A *Celebration* ensued with family, friends, courtiers, and fellow Chevaliers throughout nearly a week of feasting, music, and general gaiety. After a week of unbridled enjoyment, the assemblage was treated to a brief tournament of Chevaliers in mock battle and horse-warrior skills.

Following his Adoubement, the future duke went about his duties as captain of the guard at Cnobheresburg while ministering to his family, particularly his precious Lady Cnobheresburg. They would eventually be blessed with three children, starting with the eldest daughter, Lady Diot, just a few years old during his captaincy of the guard. The Duke prayed that he'd be worthy of his new station in life that was rapidly approaching, his high responsibility for his castle, its lands, and their kingdom at large.

After my rise to Knighthood, it came to me how I could be an example of the Arthurian-based Order of Excalibur notion I contemplated on two grounds. First, it just might put me on better terms with Bishop Hardewood about my worthiness for the Dukedom.

Second, it would also show him my dedication to practically train future Knights after I would ascend to my dad's position following eventual his death. The Order of Excalibur would certainly, at least, show the Lord my dedication to His will for my life by leading his fiefdom in His name.

Chapter Six

FAMILY

"When it bleeds, it pours," an old sage once told me after I survived my first encounter with the Danish Norsemen sometime before our Mercian problem.

I and my family were taking a well-deserved rest after my forces overcame the Mercian forces. It had been nearly a month since that terrible battle, but sometimes, it felt like yesterday, with my wounds still healing.

His best buddy, the male mastiff called Samson, nearly 225 pounds of devotion and protection, lay at his feet. Samson's mate Delilah, a bit smaller at 180 pounds, jealously guarded her little brood and the Keep. His Duchess of Cnobheresburg was off visiting family and friends now that there was some peace in the land.

And a good thing, too, for I always hesitate to let my Duchess see the distress on my visage. I feel ... very responsible for my love's good nature, and tell myself not to muck it up with my miseries. Old Samson keeps me on my toes, along with my son and our Chevaliers.

"Hail, Milord father," his son, the Marquis Aldus Benedict von Hohensee, greeted him as he entered. He was accompanied by his elder sister, Lady Diot Benedict von Hohensee, who managed never to have a hair out of place, with her light-brown curls framing a youthful countenance one might not suspect was touched by makeup. Her beauty was enhanced by her stature, standing about 5-foot 11-inches, towering over most of her contemporaries, and weighing in at nearly 150-pounds.

Lady Diot's blue eyes warned any person not to anger her or get on her wrong side. That observation was practiced by her through looking innocently at someone, then shifting her gaze to allow her to seemingly probe another's inner defenses and offenses. It sometimes put persons ill at ease, but she usually reassured them by joking how her father, the Duke of Cnobheresburg, tried to train her for Knighthood, until mother, the Duchess, finally intervened. But she often finds that searching gaze useful on different occasions.

By contrast, her youngest sibling, Lady Kiaborough Benedict von Hohensee, was not intended to be a powerhouse of strength to rival any Chevalier in her father's fiefdom, especially with a wooden sword during Squire training after she sneaks in. She appeared on the arm of her beauteous sister like she was the focus of everyone's attention, in a grown-up child fashion. Her red hair was a flaming expression of both the Duchess's warmth and directness, and her father's firmness of intention.

At 5-foot 2-inches, weighing in at a mere 110 pounds, she appears as a demure little girl overshadowed by her much taller and elder sister, and her Duke-to-be brother. She holds her own because she never gives a hint of the sleuth in the closet that wants to ferret out any secret, lie, or otherwise supposed hidden gem that could be of value to the Hohensees. Not that she's ever up to no good, but she can insinuate herself into her polite society of the day to be at once a sweet little girl, aspiring Knight, and unrelenting discoverer of the hidden.

"So grand to see you all here before me. But your mother is off on another of her tours to friends and family. I told her escorts to guard her well or face me before any tournament could be organized." The Duke seemed bubbling over with genuine good feeling.

The Duke and his small entourage of family and Knights escort made way to an area just outside their castle where they could enjoy one of the premiere sports of the day, Falconing.

"But in the meantime, peradventure," the Duke continued, "we should try out my son's latest airborne hunter, his beauteous Falcon called Nadine."

The bird took off from the Marquis' left arm, which was well clad with leather gloves with wide cuffs to withstand his prized Falcon's talons. His Nadine took to the sky like the majestic winged creature she was, so far and fast she seemed like some spirit-chaser to the Heavens. But in the blink of an eye, Nadine came rushing back to earth, though not, as they first thought, in a hurry to roost. She had better things on her mind: the rodent about to be her lunch.

After Nadine's display of savagery and grace, the Hohensees returned indoors to a more welcoming part of their castle and arrayed themselves around a comforting fire, while the wind outside played soothing melodies. The ease of familiarity emboldened the family to drop their guard—though only a little—so as not to be *en garde* on an occasion free of threat.

The Duke's family and the mastiffs were joined by their court musicians playing instrumental tunes softly in the background for the family's relaxation. They enjoyed one of the few occasions for mirth of late, and for now, memories of unpleasant times faded into near oblivion as they revived familial ties for, finally, some hoped-for peace of mind.

Chapter Seven

THE STRAIN

For years, it seemed to the now Duke Hohensee of Cnobheresburg that he wasn't...quite there...when it came to his duties in East Anglia as a leader of a family, an aristocratic ruler in Medieval East Anglia, supporting a community of diverse persons, and...a follower of his God, Jesus.

How do I reconcile oneself to being a killer of men in defending one's homeland, a preserver of peace in God's name, and still be regarded as a decent human being, even as I scratched my Sampson's head and chin?

The Duke recalled how now Bishop Hardewood and he were engaged in many verbal sparing matches over the Duke's carrying out his Knight's pledge and kingdom ruler responsibilities. The minister implied the duke's lack of sufficiency for God's blessings for him and East anglia. In answer to that issue, the Duke found himself confronting time and again: what does the Lord require of me, as he recalled from Deuteronomy 10:12 from, the Bible's Old Testament?

"Bishop Hardewood, as my direct conduit to the Lord through Mass and Confession, how do I improve my faithful performance of duty? What can I do, my honorable minister, to not only assure myself of rightful actions to the Lord, but for the people I rule, too?" the Duke asked with some noteble frustration.

"My dear Duke. only God knows the sure path yee seek. Far be it from me to stand in the Lord's stead to direct your actions," the Bishop advocated.

"That's where I'm troubled, my holy father," the Duke responded. "YOU are my human connection with God, so I look TO YOU to guide me, my dear father," he continued.

"What you need, my dear duke, is trusting in the good will of the lord to get you through. By the way, Mass tonight at even. shor ta see ya there?" as the bishop waves good-bye.

THAT'S what I'm tryin' to enable myself to do...except for not gettin' real support from His excellency, the Bishop.

Chapter Eight

VISITATION

The Duchess of Cnobheresburg wondered about how to reveal her fears to her fiercest supporter and confidante, her sister, the Duchess of Elham.

The coach, of a type known as a *Chariot Branlant*, was made with a chain suspension for smoother rides. It had an overhead cover and doors, and was drawn by four horses. Most nobles, and certainly the Duke, appointed their coach with a driver and footman at the front, with another footman riding on the rear.

The Chariot Branlant was decorated, as was customary, with the noble's colors and coat-of-arms. But the Duchess of Cnobheresburg also wondered what the commoners thought when they saw the Hohensee coat-of-arms, representing Castle Burgh and Cnobheresburgh, roll through their land? She knew that many of them had fought with the Duke against the Mercians a month-and-a-half ago in early Spring. But she felt concern for those who had survived the battle and for the welfare of those who had lost loved ones.

Their journey's end drew near, for she spied the chimneys of Elham, with Castle Rising nearby. Soon the rear footman would dismount to pull down the steps from the coach's underbelly so she and her ladies could safely exit their vehicle.

Another coach for this gathering had brought Lady Ella Chestney of Dunwich from Framlington Castle with her ladies in waiting, Semmence Brangwin and Elysande Norma, and another transported Marchioness Adelaide Oswick of Dereham from Denton Castle with her ladies in waiting Dionisia Frankland and Edeva Campion.

"Why, my Duchess Cnobheresburg, you don't look a day over your last year's age, I'll warrant," commented her sister, the Duchess Regina Cristina of Elham. "I'll add a cheer for your Duke's success against those butchers, the Mercians. Oh … I'm sorry, you poor dear, how is your Duke? Is he doing better after that awful battle with the Mercians?" her sister added, making a greater show of compassion.

The Duchess of Cnobheresburg managed a smile even as the truth sunk in about the battle's consequences. "He's … well, he'll pull through. He always does," she commented half-heartedly with a sniffle, as her lady-in-waiting Evaine offered her a handkerchief and her arm.

"Ladies, I think it's time for us all to settle in here at Elham and prepare for a wonderful gathering. We'll attend Mass in our chapel in the morning with Bishop Elia Thaderos. We haven't had such a lively gathering in … who knows how long? And how about a good bath, hey? I'll gather my kitchen maids and laundresses to draw hot water from my main cook fire for your tubs. Your ladies in waiting may provide your linen sleepwear after you've finished. I'll also have bedpans (i.e., with hot embers or hot sand) under your bed sheets to help keep you warm," she offered. Then the Duchess of Elham clapped her hands for her staff to begin bathing preparations. Her ladies-in-waiting, Celestria Dumont and Anais Bauldry, led their illustrious visitors to their soothing baths.

After the visiting ladies enjoyed their luxurious baths, each was led to her own chamber for a night's rest. The Duchess of Cnobheresburg called for Evaine to propose a special project.

"Keep me aware of what's said around our comfy station here, and out in the commons, but…quietly, OK? I Want to stay ahead of the talk so I'll know how to speak to my Duke about what's really going on in our realm. You'll be my…second set of eyes and ears.

We need all the help we can get. May I count on you?"

"I feel that there would be interest in others knowing—from a woman's view—what life was like for high-born ladies and their servants during this troubled era in our history," the Duchess of Cnobheresburg explained.

"But m'lady! How could I do what is reserved for persons as yaself, not a … servant, begging your pardon, my Duchess?" Lady Evaine tried to dissuade her patron.

"I'll not hear of ya leaving from ya new duty to me, my dear Evaine. I chose ya to be among my servants because ya were bright and made a good show of yaself when ya were a little girl. I knew ya parents and promised them I'd look after ya when they died in that Danish Viking surprise attack some time ago. It was horrible, but we at least saved ya and a few others when my Duke came to rescue ya. You've proven ya worth and subsequent duty to me ever since. Besides, I know ya're good at language and of speaking with persons of different callings," the Duchess of Cnobheresburg told her.

"All right, my Duchess. I'm at ya service as always," Lady Evaine agreed.

Lady Ashdown joined them to help the Duchess get settled in for the night, with an assortment of fine linens to choose from for her slumber.

Chapter Nine

ESCORT

The Duchess of Elham's people of Castle Rising also made accommodations for the ladies' entourage of escorts, each having a *lance fournie*—a quartet of Knights—as their protectors. Four came from Burgh Castle with the Duchess of Cnobheresburg, adorned in their purple and gray vestments, cloaks, and accoutrements such as spurs, sweord, shield, lance, helmet, and gloves, as did their fellow Knights. Four more Knights, in the brown and yellow livery of Denton Castle, escorted the Marchioness Adelaide of Dereham, and another four looked after Lady Ella of Dunwich, Knights in red and black. Finally, there were the four knights from Castle Rising in their green and orange livery who were assigned to look after their Duchess of Elham.

"May I introduce you, my comrades-in-arms, to an evening of mead and refreshments?" offered Sir Ricar of the Castle Rising escort. "We won't get drunk enough to miss Mass in the morning, my comrade Chevaliers. Let's work out the watch details for our *mesdames* and *mademoiselles* for this evening so that there'll be at least one of us en garde around our trusts at all times. So who's up for a not-so-boring evening of ladies' conversations, *mes amis*?" Sir Ricar finished.

"All's well and good for us," chimed in Sir Leofwin on behalf of himself and his comrades from Castle Burgh. "I'll be among the first watch. We're under strict orders to be at our Duchess's beck and without fail. The Duke of Cnobheresburg has sworn us to guard his Duchess with our lives and sacred honor," Sir Leofwin explained.

"Well, before you go off to another grand adventure for these powerful ladies, let's have a toast to our comradeship in this great realm of East Anglia," said another of Lady Ella Chestney's Dunwich Knights. "Let's be off to Castle Rising's keep for our bedding down, my kind sirs—except for those on duty for the moment," Sir Euric added.

The Knights congratulated one another by clasping forearms as their sign of comradeship, much like their Roman forebearers of long ago.

Sir Ricar of Castle Rising, Sir Leofwine of Burgh Castle, Sir Leofric of Denton Castle, and Sir Childabert of Framlington Castle reported to the upper story of Castle Rising near Elham.

The first Lance Fournie of protective guards for their high-born female charges from around East Anglia made fast their posts, while each of their ladies settled down after a meal with their host, the Duchess of Elham.

Following this group of Knights to be en garde were Sir Godwin of Burgh Castle, Sir Adalbert of Denton Castle, Sir Ode of Framlington Castle, and Sir Gararic of Castle Rising. Their quarters were sparse but adequate, with cots, stuffed straw mats, and lumpy pillows. Each knight was soon fast asleep, but they also had learned to keep an eye open for danger even in a civil location like Castle Rising.

After each lance fournie completed its night duty, there was the daylight mission to accomplish. "So how do we want to do our duty during the daylight, my comrades?" asked Sir Donnchad of Denton Castle.

"I propose we continue with four-hour rotations of duty day and night, as we started last night," Sir Grimwald of Castle Rising put in.

"Sounds about right to me. What say we vote on it? Or pull straws? Just how do we get agreement on this little adventure?" said Sir Gerold of Framlington Castle.

"Why don't we simply agree to put in our time as we've started, rotating every four hours? By the way, this kind of schedule allows us some free time to train and keep ourselves in shape while being genteel around our ladies," suggested Sir Charibert of Denton Castle.

"I knew you were a man after my own heart, *mon Chevalier*. Let's do it, in the name of our liege lords and their ladies," bellowed Sir Sigisbert of Castle Rising.

Sir Sigisbert's outburst led them all into a raucous cacophony of sounds—not exactly singing, but as knightly seasoned warriors, it served them well to affirm acceptance of the plan for their guard duty.

Altogether, the lance fournie of Knights from the participating Ladies' escorts were: from Burg Castle with Sirs Godwin, Leofwine, Wealdhere, and Wynnstan in purple-n-grey livery; from Castle Rising with Sirs Grimwald, Gararic, Ricar, and Sigisbert in green-n-orange; from Castle Dunwich with Sirs Euric, Hrothulf, Mærwine, and Tata in red-n-black livery; Castle Denton with Sirs Adalbert, Cheribert, Donnchad, and Leofric in brown-n-yellow; and Castle Framlington with Sirs Sir Childabert, Sir Æbbe, Sir Ode, and Sir Gerold with blue-n-white.

Chapter Ten
SOCIAL

Rising before sunrise, the Duchess of Elham and her servants prepared the morning's repast for her honored guests. It usually consisted of stiff bread and wine. Sometimes, there would be fruits from the peasant gardens, and maybe, once in a while, some other grain foods. After this initial ladies' gathering, the Duchess of Elham then conducted her guests to their chapel, where her Bishop Thaderos performed Mass. The entourage of visiting Knights were there, too.

With their worship of the Lord completed, as was the custom of most high-born of the people of East Anglia, the Ladies repaired to a small chamber off the main hall that was aglow with a roaring fireplace and plenty of comforters and cushioned seats. There was also one Knight from each lady's home castle discreetly stationed within sight and sound of their charge, yet not listening to their private intonations. That was another aspect of their Code of Conduct: to be discreet, compassionate, and loyal, especially towards women and children.

The Duchess of Elham got the conversation going. "So, my Ladies, besides a needed repast for great conversation, we need to discuss Lady Diot's wedding. It can't be put off much longer if the suitable match with the Earl of Bury St. Edmunds is to be realized for the stability of our land. Besides, St. Andrews Castle is a good fortification and refuge in times of peril. Not that your Lady Diot will always hold up there, seeing as how you and your daughter are close," the Duchess of Elham enticed her sister lovingly.

"Yes, I know it must be done, but ... does she have to marry this—this *dimwit* of a high-born in our land? I mean, really, only he is available to her?" the Duchess of Cnobheresburg confessed her view of this necessary deal for the kingdom. "If God would only make this a different miracle for a more ... *pleasing* husband."

"But think about this way. In time, you'll have an heir—or two or three—to continue the line of Hohensee in this era of uncertainty and realm difficulties," the Duchess of Elham chided her younger sister,.

"Well, I hope they don't act or think as uninvitingly as their father the Earl," the Duchess Cnobheresburg replied.

"Ladies, our repast is ready. So let's get down to some serious dickering about this hopefully happy event for Norfolk and Suffolk. Lady Celestria, would you mind bringing in those bolts of fabric? I may now show my sister what's available for a great wedding gown, and of course wearables for the ball and other socials after the wedding," she ordered.

When Celestria returns with the cloth fabrics, the Ladies continue their counsel about Lady Diot's wedding wardrobe.

Lady Evaine was joined by Lady Anais as they sought to do as they were bidden. Lady Evaine had taken care of being sure everyone was there who should be. Lady Anais also did her part to be sure the repast was available.

When the bread and wine were given to everyone's fill, the Ladies got down to real business.

"Who really is this Earl of Bury St. Edmunds?" the Marchioness Adelaide asked politely, if with a slight humorous laugh.

"Oh you poor dear, my Lady Adelaide. You haven't heard? He's the hero of nearly every encounter with our would-be conquerors, to hear him describe it. Astride his gallant steed, he almost single-handedly saved the day for East Anglia's forces. It's a wonder that the Duke of Cnobheresburg could not have used his forces' help on his side of that epic battle. I just shiver thinking of how much better that battle could have gone if the Lord and mighty Earl of St. Bury Edmunds could have added even more to our side's victory," said Lady Ella of Dunwich, an up and coming noble person, added to the building mirth.

"Ladies, Ladies. Let's be thankful we may find some use for the Earl of St. Bury Edmunds," the Duchess of Elham jumped in. "You know there needed to be heirs for future ruler vacancies. Maybe he'll be ...you know, pretty good in bed—even if he can't prove himself on the field of honor, championing our realm," she added with relish.

"Umm ...I wonder what he'd be like, y'know, where it counts?" offered the Marchioness Adelaide with a shy smile.

"All right, Ladies. Let's not eviscerate the poor dear before he has a chance to prove himself in God's sight, and with his bride to be. Even with our star bride-to-be not being here, we may do her justice by helping arrange what we think will do her justice for her wedding. We haven't had so glorious a celebration in a while, ladies," the Duchess of Elham was saying.

"But speaking of our star of this trip, how's she doing since she didn't join us?" the Duchess added.

"She'd rather stay home and attend her father, who seemed to barely survive … that recent battle," the Duchess of Cnobheresburg acknowledged with some obvious emotional difficulty.

"So sorry, my sister. It must be hard on you. Please take comfort among those here who feel your pain and wish the best for you and your family. Ya'r Duke is a sterling example of the Knights' Code of Conduct, and his Order of Excalibur pledge after his Knighting. Let us surround you with our love and devotion. You know we feel much of what you're going through. Rest yaself among friends and relatives," the Duchess of Elham comforted her sister.

"Say, I almost forgot. We have a new member of our circle of Ladies to promote. Yes, Lady Ella of Dunwich is being elevated to the rank of Marchioness by imperial decree of the East Anglian nobles, in recognition of her selfless efforts to serve her home fief, Dunwich. She also looked after the family during a close call with some Mercians who wandered near Framlington Castle during that recent battle.

"Oh, my gawd, ladies! We've got to get ready for the midday meal. My Ladies will help you get dressed. And we'll have some guests arriving. Just some local dealers from Elham and such. It's time, Ladies, to don your best dress for the occasion. We'll finalize Lady Diot's wedding and dowry later on," the Duchess of Elham said.

Chapter Eleven

HEALING

"All right, my dear children—oh—" the Duke of Cnobheresburg caught himself. "Forgive me, my heirs. I sometimes forget that I can't bounce you all on my knees anymore. Well!" he continued, "let's be about our family, eh? Pass the Meade and some of that mutton, will ye?" he invited them.

They all started laughing like the family they used to be before the wars with the Danes and the Mercians. "I'll bet you could eat a horse, my pappa, huh? If you didn't prefer him as your war companion," his younger daughter, the Lady Kiaborough, said, laughing out loud. It then became a free-for-all laugh fest as all present coalesced into the family they had always been. Even Samson barked periodically, as if to answer questions not directed to him.

After much joking and good-natured fun befitting a royal family at peace with themselves, the impromptu fun fest dwindled until only the Marquis and the Duke remained. "It was a great evening for us all, being together for a change, my father. So now let's get going on what needs to be done rather shortly if we're to maintain good standing," the Marquis said quite seriously between bouts of wooziness from the Mead they all consumed.

"Yes, I know," answered the Duke. "I must embark upon a different kind of campaign now to get your elder sister properly wedded to the right suitor—the *right* suitor…" The Duke paused, seeming to ponder his own need for action. "It's my role as a Duke to work out kingdom agreements that will help ensure the welfare of my fief, but … I'm also … a father, and I love all my children, no matter their current ages," he finished with some emotional difficulty.

I've got to keep myself together with my son and not let the Meade speak for me... though...that is kinda hard to do...right now...

"Yes, father, I know," said the Marquis in empathy with both his Liege and his father. "But it's got to be done. We both know that. You can delay such an arrangement no longer, my father. Your kingdom awaits your decision," his son added with an encouraging air of sympathy.

Chapter Twelve

WEDDING

The joining of my eldest daughter, the Lady Diot, to the Earl of Bury St. Edmunds, is soon upon us. I will describe what was hoped to be a very joyous occasion for the realm of East Anglia. My Duchess Cnobheresburg had recently returned from her visit with the Duchess of Elham, her sister. Late Spring came upon the East Anglian countryside like expected candlelight in the darkness of night—a ray of hopeful beaming into a new day of promises kept. It was also after our victory earlier in this season against the Mercians. The Danes were not expected to be an issue until the next year.

They had gathered at the long table on the opposite side of their chapel to talk about the wedding. "I hope to reveal some details on the ceremony to come," the Duke of Cnobheresburg said and stood up.

"The dowry for Lady Diot should have been sufficient for the Earl of St. Bury Edmunds, since they certainly could use it. I provided a team of war horses, a goodly amount of gold coin, and a seat on the East Anglia council, approved by all the current members between Norfolk and Suffolk. But of course, if the Earl of Bury St. Edmunds doesn't really need those horses in support of his cadre of Knights ... well, I'll surely find some use for them," the Duke explained with a humorous twist.

What with Bury St. Edmund's stables nearly in shambles, and their peasant crops showing the lowest yield in many decades, we wanted to be forthcoming, as well as compassionate toward our future son-in-law. Yet my dear Duchess of Cnobheresburg insisted that we be generous. After all, the Duchess reminded me, we're not losing a daughter as much as we're gaining added security for ourselves and surrounding fiefs with a greater militia commitment.

Amazing! What a brilliant negotiator my Duchess has turned out to be—for our benefit. I know Lady Diot is in good hands under her mother's sagacity. My daughter will always look out for her family home and will continue to be a good asset for our continued success. It was a fine day in late June for a wedding, and our plans for this necessary gala event, were about to manifest. The church at Cnobheresburg was again the site of resplendent ceremony for all concerned.

The Lady Diot was resplendent in her flowing gown of white with gray highlights and attached hood. Her auburn hair was attractively arrayed along her forehead and face like a newfound portrait of the Lady she was. She was ably escorted into the hall by her beaming father, appropriately attired in the livery of his station as the Duke of Cnobheresburg, with purple and gray highlighting his coat-of-arms.

With a blare of trumpets, the groom made his entrance, followed by his entourage of sycophants and lackeys worthy of his station for a future kingdom in England. But for now, he was hard to miss, dressed in his finest livery, with yellow and green crushed-velvet pants, flowery shirt, brocade vest, floppy hat, and knee boots. His Honor the groom, Earl of Bury St. Edmunds, seemed to draw everyone's attention, as surely was his intent.

When all the principals were gathered at the stand before the Bishop of Cnobheresburg, all conversation became mute. His Eminence, Bishop Hardewood, began his ceremonial banter of bringing the two betrothed together in holy matrimony. When the ceremony was completed, the green-eyed former Lady Diot of Cnobheresburg had become the Marchioness Diot of Beodrivesworth. She would shortly move to take up her new station in the kingdom but would endeavor to monitor and influence events at her former home as best she could.

Meanwhile, the Duke of Cnobheresburg, still a bit teary-eyed from all the festivities surrounding his eldest child's wedding, managed a clear thought about the border between his fiefdom, the Danes, and the Mercians. But soon he chastised himself for daring to cloud an otherwise beautiful day. *It's done. It's done. One less thing to worry about … I hope.*

Later that day, the Duke and his son looked to another venture. "Do you think it's a good stand to hold a major tournament so soon after my sister's wedding, Milord father?" Marquis Aldus questioned. "Not to take away from our Chevaliers' readiness to joust, but allowances must be made for their absence to visit families and see to various needs in their respective holdings. After all, latter Spring is their long-awaited rest time before warm-weather, Summer wars, loom again for us," the captain of the Duke's host explained.

His father pondered his son's notions before answering. "If I were yet a pagan, I could be persuaded to sacrifice to the gods to ensure a good outcome for this coming battle season. But the Lord Jesus will come through for us. In the meantime, let's be about our tournament, my captain, eh?" the Duke cajoled his son.

Over the next few weeks, attendees for the tournament would assemble at the Duke of Cnobheresburg's tournament grounds, a mile or so west of Burgh Castle.

Chapter Thirteen

EXCALIBUR

By sponsoring this tourney, I'm also underscoring the connection between Charlemagne's Code of Ethics for Chivalry, and the fabled adventures of King Arthur and his Round Table of Knights and the sword of valor, Excalibur. I see the history the Code and my Order of Excalibur working together to solidify our kingdom of Knights in meeting head-on the onslaughts of the Mercians and the Danes.

"Now that we are at peace—for now," said the Duke of Cnobheresburg after pacing about his audience chamber, "it's time to get on with Chevalier training for our young Squires and Pages before they think they already know what it is to be a Chevalier." The Duke laughed out loud. "So let's be about it, my captain," he ordered, with a nod from his son.

About a dozen lads and lassies were awaiting their turn at various wooden training devices. Starting at age six, they came from neighboring castles aligned with the Duke of Cnobheresburg and East Anglia. The girls, of course, would be accorded extra concern, as they were not necessarily expected to be Chevaliers, as their parents' concerns for marriage and related court issues took precedence. But Ladies knowing their way around a sword were better prepared for any eventuality in this troubling world. By the age of twelve, the Pages were expected to have mastered a lot of the sciences, court mannerisms and behaviors, and rudimentary skills in horsemanship, archery, fencing, spear-handling, and military strategizing. When the girls successfully made it to being Squire and beyond, they would then be Knighted and addressed as Dame with their first or given name. The lads were addressed as Sir with their given name only after being Knighted.

Along their matriculation to be a Chevalier, each candidate would develop strong spiritual, mental, and physical well-roundedness to accord each the strength and integrity to be courteous, faithful (to God, family, and one's Liege lord), accountable, and expert Chevaliers. Their dual moral and ethical fortitude takes its calling from Holy Scripture's concept of the Trinity—Father, Son, and Holy Spirit—as revealed in Genesis 1:26 by the involvement of the Elohim (Hebrew for the Trinity) with Creation.

Additional emphasis was placed on the Pages and Squires being versed in the literature of the day, like the tales of King Arthur and the Round Table. These children were expected to build a durable awareness of the Chevalier's way of life to help them become fully immersed in it. Other challenges to be mastered included swimming, hunting, poem-writing for the lady or gentleman of one's heart, and chess. Becoming a Chevalier was never easy, but it attainable if the Squire made it through their start as a Page.

A ruler's sponsorship of a tournament allows aspiring Chevaliers to demonstrate their availability to serve as Knights. Those who would be Knights are also gifted with a display of experience as a Chevalier—they witness firsthand knights in action on horseback as on the field of battle.

Becoming a Chevalier is an honor within the feudal community. A ruler's tournament allows him—or her—to show off their Knights' skills while also introducing novices to the life they wish to emulate. Novices display what they've learned, while battle-hardened Knights show how it's really done.

Chapter Fourteen
DEATHWATCH

"We have a lot to prepare for our tournament coming up soon, my son," the Duke of Cnobheresburg spoke in a voice not greater than a whisper to Marquis Aldus. "Maybe I'm a little tired," he admitted, trying to steady himself on the edge of his chair of office after standing up with noticeable fatigue.

"Father! Give yourself a little breathing space to ... rest a bit more, so you'll be in great form for the tourney," his son the Marquis said. "We could delay it a bit longer to be sure of your stirring presence, which will give all of us that sense of invincibility we achieved against the Mercians and the Danes. Let your people see you as the strong leader you are. They need you, my father, the Duke of Cnobheresburg, to stand up strongly and proudly as our glorious leader."

Indeed, there was an urgency—one that would affect the outcome of not only Chevalier training but the rule of the realm itself.

The Duke was dying.

I'm telling no one of the extent of my injuries. Such intimacy and candor I can not afford to give to anyone not directly connected to me and mine. How do I reveal my mortality in so many words? But more importantly, how do I prepare my family even as I'm working towards this needed tournament? Tourneys, after all, help ensure worthy Squires and Knights are prepared for their coveted roles in this society.

I am, though, preparing--in secret—to find the best way to prepare my son, the Marquis, for his eventual ascendency to rule. But how do I prepare the love of my life, my beauteous Duchess, for such a loss to her, and our children?

Over the next few weeks as the Summer Solstice approached, when the breezes were blustery but soothing on the skin, little more than half the original aspirants remained as Squires. The Squires had to show their absolute acceptance of the Knights' code of conduct, also known as the Chivalric Code. A good reminder of their Knightly pursuit manifested through remembrances of the legendary King Arthur tales vested in the Order of Excalibur.

This noteworthy ethic of horse-warrior behavior enabled the Chevalier to observe and demonstrate a Code of Conduct that prescribed putting in practice such ideals as bravery, courtesy, honor, and gallantry towards women. With the ideals of Chivalry in mind, able Squires took part in tourneys to help them display their accomplished skills as Chevaliers. But it wasn't until the experienced Chevaliers put on their displays of warrior skills in tourneys that all aspirants could envision their sought-after future.

Among the challenges were a mêlée—French for a confused crush of activity—between two groups of Chevaliers who charged and fought so as to appear to be a disorganized rabble. In jousting, a pair of Chevaliers charged each other in a one-on-one contest, with a safety block on the lance's point. Other exhibitions involved the Chevaliers' accuracy with archery and lances against stationary targets. The tournament lasted a day or two, with totals of wins and losses spurring greater camaraderie and fellowship among the Chevaliers and Squires.

Chapter Fifteen

TOURNAMENT

Streamers festooned the Duke's arena, conjuring such Chevalier grandeur as could be by a ruler who was given to properly prepare Pages and Squires for their future roles as Knights.

On that Summery morning in the year of our Lord in August 805, the Duke, his family, far and distant rulers in East Anglia, neighboring villagers and commoners, and of course sellers of whatever merchandise they could muster were all in attendance for what could amount to a blood-fest of Knightly skills and daring.

First up to cajole the spectators with derring-do were Squire prospects plying their skills on foot against stationary targets bearing different coat-of-arms. "I'll bet ya couldn't shoot the small side of a wall, yer Knightly sir," called out a commoner tasked to aid the Squires and Pages with their preparation for competition. This usual teasing commentary made the rounds for all the Squires to bear. It would have been very telling of the Squire's fortitude to be a Knight if he couldn't take the ribbing.

"Ah, come on, liddle one," said another aide-de-camp to a short and seemingly out-of-place Page who sought to bring refreshment to his assigned Knight or Squire. "You caun't bear that wee bit of wine with your liddle fngers, short one?" He then proceeded to kick his feet from under him. But the Page was rescued by an understanding Squire, who kicked the crap out of that renegade peasant and called him a bully.

"Hear ye! Hear ye!" blares the tournament's herald for all festivities. "Thanks to the gracious permission of his majesty, the Duke of Cnobheresburg, we will entertain, beguile, and demonstrate the art and savagery of Knighthood, without wanton violence or disgrace from any of the participants.

"We will offer titling, or jousts, between equally capable Chevaliers. There will also be tests of skills in archery, spear-throwing, and sword-handling. And yes, my hungry gathering: with the blessings of our dear Liege, the Duke of Cnobheresburg, our Pages are eager to show what they've learned. By the way, the main jousts will feature Squires in their first armor-fitting suits for mock combat ahorse.

"I now present you with our Liege, who will give the signal for this tournament in action," finished the herald in the first of many pronouncements.

As the ruler of East Anglia, I still am shocked by the sheer ferocity of Knights engaging in mock combat through their jousts, leaving some crashing to the ground like discarded trash, others bereft of an arm or leg, with still others dead. If you could bear to look, you'd see lances piercing shield and Knight, swords beheading a Knight, or two combatants crashing into each other across the titling divider.

The lesson to be learned here, of course, is to be the victor, not the vanquished. I say it quietly to myself, though, unable to say or show favoritism it to the Squires and Pages having to undergo this tragedy. They help to clear the grounds of bloody bodies, body parts, horses severely wounded, and the entire scene of Knights' training in preparation for real combat. What an introduction to the Order of Excalibur for youth to follow for their own defense and that of their loved ones! My Excalibur program was to enable a connection the mythical Arthurian tales of Chivalry, and the real life Knightly Code of Conduct to prepare them a future of life as a horse-warrior for Christ.

Tournaments like these are the better way—so far—to carry out my motives for my Knightly retinue.

Chapter Sixteen

GIFTING

"Things went very well for our tournament, my son," said the Duke of Cnobheresburg to the Marquis Aldus. "Would you agree?" the Duke sought to banter with his son and heir.

"Yes, my father, the tournament did indeed go well … except … you seemed overly mirthful this time around. Is there some … *notion* that's taken a hold of you, my Liege?" his son implored.

"Now, now my good son and captain," the Duke said sheepishly. "I wouldn't want to spoil the surprise I've arranged. So let's just say you'll be very gratified when it's ready," he added to silence his son on the subject.

"So be it, my clever father. No further comments from me on that subject. I swear it." Then they both heard the horn blast, announcing a visitor to their keep.

Soon the Duke would reveal his surprise for his son, the Marquis Aldus—an unusual offering that might be best comprehended as a token rather than something tangible to hold in one's hand. *It's certain to be a welcomed gift*, or so the Duke reasoned. But he wanted to prepare his son to be his replacement in a practical way.

The day came for the Duke's gift to his son. They met privately in an anteroom of Castle Cnobheresburg, with mead-filled goblets and other refreshments to sustain them. The Duke smiled at his son, who looked back at him with a tenderness befitting a father-son relationship. They were two of a kind: ruler and ruler-to-be, and both Chevaliers.

"This is what I've been holding on to for so long, waiting for the right time. It's something you and I share as men, and not something—no blame to your mother and sisters—that women can share. So ..." The Duke unwrapped one of his special items for the Marquis. "I have this for you."

It was a bejeweled dagger, about ten inches in length, double-edged, bearing the Hohensee family colors and crest. The Marquis' first thought was that it looked expensive. He hefted the blade, recognizing not only its weight and feel in his hand but its potential for battle. "Father—" the Marquis started to say before the Duke raised his hand.

"Here's something else for you as well," his father announced with a greater gleam in his eyes. The Marquis then unwrapped another expensively wrapped package to reveal a gleaming sword.

"Mon Dieu, my Liege," was all the Marquis could manage to say. His father's second gift was an Anglo-Saxon Tang sweord, like the one he had about thirty-seven inches long, double-edged, wrought of strong steel by special procedures, with a clean hilt shaped like a cross and a scabbard with Hohensee family heraldry and colors.

"I arranged these little somethings to show you how much confidence and trust I place in you for our castle's and the people's security," the Duke explained. The Marquis looked astonished beyond words. "So what will you dub this blade of yours, my son?"

"Father ... I—I ..." His surprise gave him no words.

"Don't worry, my son," the Duke added. "You're more than qualified to have these as my token of the high trust for your valiant stand with this keep through the battles with the Danes and the Mercians. Ye will be a great ruler—as great as I am today, maybe even better ... one day!" the Duke finished with raucous laughter.

Marquis Aldus joined him in that mirthful moment. "My dear father, I shall dub this wonderful gift from you *Light-Bearer*, in that I hope to continue in your troth as the new Duke leading our people to repeated success against our would-be invaders," the Marquis extolled.

Chapter Seventeen

ANNOUNCEMENT

After the arrival of Earl and Lady Beodrivesworth, the Duke and Duchess of Cnobheresburg came to the banquet hall in noteworthy splendor befitting the occasion. It was the first public view of the newlyweds of Bury St. Edmunds Castle. It was an arena for present and future intrigue among the East Anglian aristocracy, especially between the folks at Cnobheresburg and St. Edmunds.

The Duke's remaining daughter, sometimes jokingly called Little Lady K, was there in rare form—a sometimes mincing, sometimes precocious, and always unbelievably smart teen. She undoubtedly knew the strain she put on her father, the Duke, if she did not at least appear to be on good behavior around strangers, guests, and the villagers. But nearly everybody knew that Lady K would have her day when she made it through Chevalier training. "There's something about swords and shields," she always noted, "that gets me going, like being a Viking queen or some such." Neither the Duke nor Duchess Cnobheresburg were praying and planning for that kind of future for her, but they would be patient. "Even if it kills us," they sighed together.

In company, the Earl of Beodrivesworth had a tendency to make persons ill at ease with his twisted dialogue about his supposed wartime bravado, but Lady Beodrivesworth did her best to keep things from getting out of hand. She was gifted with a great sense of humor while having a better assessment of tough situations, like the time her father made a playful pass at a service girl, not realizing that the Duchess was looking at him when as he did. It was a stupid thing for her dad—yet the Duke of this fief--to do. But she knew he was only "playing" with a servant, but such "plays" have often lead to deadly consequences for an entire family, and a disaster for a whole realm. At least in this incident, she was effectively able to help sooth her mom's—the Duches of Cnobheresburg's—feelings and sense of worth at a time of often changing and potentially harmful turmoil with the Mercian and Danish threats ever looming at the edge of her father's fief and future.

Lady Beodrivesworth planned to continue being a great arbiter for present and future engagements, especially considering her father's determination to succeed and her husband's bragging.

Lady Beodrivesworth's visit to her family's castle at Cnobheresburg remained an enjoyable circumstance. She was always on the lookout for curbing her husband's bent for laughter at the expense of others, especially high-ranking persons like her father, the Duke of Cnobheresburg. It was the family outing where Nadine and the other falcons were let loose to hunt that evening's festive serving for the banquet. Nadine performed her best, fetching two rabbits and three sparrows. She was, indeed, a champion among her breed. The other hunting birds did their share, too.

After the guests left, and their ladies had retired for the evening, the Duke and the Marquis went to their favorite spot in the castle where they could overlook the North Sea. They were quiet for a spell, then the Duke gave a brief cough.

"My son, the captain of my guard and keeper of our home," the Duke began, then hesitated. "I—uh ..."

"Father, just say what you want me to know," the Marquis said. "It can't be all that bad, my Liege?" His mind still held questions about the measure of his father's desire.

"I'm ...dying, my son ... ever so slowly, but our healers have confirmed it. I'm dying," the Duke muttered.

"Father, I—" the Marquess started to say.

His father put his hand up. "I need you to know that you'll be running the kingdom very shortly. I, uh, don't have much time, my dear son, to prepare you. You'll have no problem with assuming the title and rights and privileges that go with your running things. I ... just wanted you to know long before it becomes too obvious," the Duke explained slowly.

"My father ... I ... but you look fine. A little tired, maybe. Do the Duchess and my siblings know?" He needed to understand what was happening.

"No, I've not told them. But I will soon. I needed to prepare you first because they'll be leaning on your strength, as they have been with me. But now that you know, let's be about this tournament, my good captain!" the Duke said.

With the hoopla of the wedding now a memorable event, and the tournament plans well underway, the Duke of Cnobheresburg was now able to review the progress of the Pages and Squires towards their goal of becoming a Chevalier.

"How goes it, Milord father?" inquired the Marquis. "I've gone through the list of Chevaliers invited to participate, your Lordship. We had some Chevaliers from Kent, Essex, and Wessex as well as East Anglia. It had been a blessing for our coffers, what with the bazaar and other market goods available for sale. We are collecting many taxes from this show of chevalier skills," the captain of the Duke's host offered.

It occurred to the Duke that a great deposit of funds would enable him to finance another defense of his realm.

"I can see that our main industries, with wool and mutton from our healthy and frisky sheep and our villagers' vegetable crops, will get a boost from added sales. Then there are our horses to serve the forces of our kingdom. Our whole fiefdom, besides the Island of Flegg, will continue doing as well," the captain commented as he left to review their castle's security.

Chapter Eighteen

ENGAGEMENT

The tally of activity during the Duke of Cnobheresburg's tournament included the best in the kingdom and notable survivors of ferocious battles with the Danes and the Mercians. This year's tournament had made the Duke proud to be a ruler in East Anglia.

"By all accounts, we did rather well with our tournament, adding to our treasury more than enough funds to finance future battles against those damnable Danes and persistent Mercians," the Duke of Cnobheresburg detailed. "And then there was your sister's wedding. "My, how her fop of a husband beguiled me with his utter lack of wit and subtlety. How may a father—and ruler—be well with that kind of situation?" the Duke confided in frustration.

"But my father and my Liege, you held up well with these things, as a person befitting your respect and integrity throughout the realm. And besides, we're blessed that Lady Diot was the bride and not my younger sister, the Lady K, our little warrior," Marquis Aldus added, overcome with laughter.

The Duke nodded in agreement while letting himself enjoy this brief moment of glee.

"Now that the tournament is done, my Liege and father," said Marquis Aldus," what becomes of our plan for the future?" They had long since put aside misgivings about their continued support of to unify East Angles with the rest of Britain, especially with the ongoing furor among other East Anglican nobles, the Mercians, and the Danes.

"We could hold out against the Danes and those merciless Mercians, but how do we settle the issue of our status among the remaining Heptarchy? I mean, look at us, my Liege: we're one mighty fief, but our future is more uncertain than ever before. There is only so much we can do—alone—among the former Heptarchy realms, my father, unless you intend to...to somehow...grow an impressive army and manage more heirs to run things—"

"--My son and heir," the Duke broke in and turned to his son slowly and deliberately, "remember, we have the Lord on our side. I am no dream-maker or worker of sorcery, my son, but a plan indeed have I, and I must hurry to acquaint you with it as soon as possible. But first, let's indulge our bellies with nourishment for today's mind-stirring beginnings." They walked into their favorite family alcove in the castle.

"There is the issue, my son, of our realm being absorbed into the Mercian web of influence in the not-to-distant future. We can hold off the Mercians now, but we'll have to settle for their rule soon enough," the Duke explained.

"It's all we've got to hold on to, my son," the Duke tried to assure his heir. "It's all that's available for the future of Norfolk and Suffolk here in East Anglia ...our home," the Duke finished.

I wish I could do better to lay out my son's better future, but...besides my dying... he'll have to stand up to what's coming for him: eventual take-over by the Mercians, his siblings, his mom the Duchess elder, and...the rest of his fief. I pray for his success no matter what happenstance.

EPILOGUE

Ealdhelm Benedict von Hohensee, Duke of Cnobheresburg, has passed to his hopefully Heavenly reward. Life after the death of one of East Anglia's most beloved rulers, the elder Duke Hohensee, seemed to grind on slowly, day by day, week by week, and month by month. Wars with the Danes and the Mercians remained ever a threat not only to Castle Cnobheresburg but to the rest of East Anglia. There was even some cooperation between Cnobheresburg and Bury St. Edmunds, thanks to Lady Diot, and the ever-growing insights of Lady K, her little sister, who became quite the spy. One memorable incident will show her value.

It was a clear day, with bluish skies and white, puffy clouds bestride the hills, forests, and dales of East Anglia around Castle Cnobheresburg. Little Lady K managed to ingratiate herself into the "inner caverns" of Chevalier status to find out tasty bits of information about courtly life, particularly the latest gossip about who, what, when, and where.

Fully armed with her bravado and just a touch of feigned shyness, Lady K pretended ignorance of courtly customs to allow a given person's confidence security not to be alarmed. And what tidbits she gathered! Thankfully, revealed only to her sister, Lady Diot.

Little Lady K and Lady Diot had remained close, especially after their father's death. That also proved to be an asset to the younger Duke of Cnobheresburg, their brother, who now rules his fief as one of many still independent realms in East Anglia.

One nice notion came to the younger Duke of Cnobheresburg from his little sister's conniving and secretive endeavors. It led to the undoing of a plot to take over Cnobheresburg by some interested third-party persons among the Mercians. The incident was thoroughly investigated, and leaders of the coup were punished with death by beheading. Lady K was unofficially applauded for her espionage efforts by her brother, the younger Duke of Cnobheresburg, and her sister, the Lady Diot of Bury St. Edmunds.

The new Duke of Cnobheresburg ended his day, like so many other rounds of the castle and the nearby village, by quietly settling at a table on the periphery of the pub, where he could be somewhat inconspicuous and yet be a part of the crowd.

The innkeeper brought over his order—a tankard of Meade, meats, cheese, and bread—then asked, "M'lawd," he asked quietly, "how else may I serve ye this fine evenin', m'lawd?" the innkeeper added. "Ah … so … I knew your father. He was a kind and gendle man but a fierce warrior. Beggin' your pardon, yer lordship, but … are ya doing all right?"

The Duke of Cnobhresburg briefly looked up at the innkeeper, smiled, and then said, "I thank you for your service to my father and me. Please … I just want a little peace before I return to the castle. But sharing this time among my people is one of the best ways to continue to honor my father's legacy," the Duke explained.

GLOSSARY

Aldus Benedict von Hohensee was the Marquis of Cnobheresburg, middle child of the Duke of Cnobheresburg, then Duke after father's death. **Lady Diot Benedict von Hohensee** of Cnobheresburg then **Marchioness Diot of Beodrivesworth,** eldest child of von Hohensee. **Lady Kiaborough Benedict von Hohensee** of Cnobheresburg, youngest child.

Bishop Aran Hardewood was Bishop of Burgh Castle and the Cnobheresburg vicinity. **Bishop Elia Thaderos** was the Bishop of Castle Rising and the Elham vicinity.

Chariot Branlant, a passenger covered wagon, was made with a chain suspension for smoother rides. It had an overhead cover and doors, and was drawn by four horses.

Charlemagne, the Frankish ruler of Europe, a member of the Carolingian dynasty, developed the Code of Conduct for Chevaliers. Chevalier was the French version of for a Knight as a mounted horse warrior. Charles Martel, who was Charlemagne's grandfather, taught Charles the Great to be a decent and respectful leader and warrior.

Code of Conduct, which embodies the Chivalric Code, was Charlemagne's insight into establishing good Christlike behavior for mounted warriors that emphasized the will to obey God and the will to work by God's design, as well as properly loving and respecting women and children.

Ealdhelm Benedict von Hohensee was the former Duke of Cnobheresburg. **Gwenllian Meliora von Hohensee** was the Duchess of Cnobheresburg.

En Garde is a defensive stance, as in the sport and the weaponry of Fencing.

Evaine Beringar and **Gisela Ashdown,** Ladies-n-Waiting for the Duchess of Cnobheresburg. **Semmence Brangwin** and **Elysande Norma**, Ladies-n-Waiting for **Lady Ella Chestney of Dunwich.**

Heptarchy was the former conglomerate of seven realms situated in England's southeast corner: Kent, East Anglia, Essex, Mercia, Northumbia, Sussex, and Wessex.

King Arthur and His Knights of the Round Table was a fictional literary account of Knights as they lived with their Code of Conduct, also known as the Chivalric Code.

Knight was a skilled horse warrior—a *Chevalier*--who followed Jesus and a Code of Conduct forged by Charlemagne.

Lance Fournie was a formation of four Knights. LFs for the ladies here were from: Castle Burg, purple-n-grey; Castle Denton, brown-n-yellow; Castle Dunwich, red-n-black; Castle Framlington, blue-n-white; and Castle Rising, green-n-orange.

Marchioness Adelaide Oswick of Dereham, with her Ladies-n-Waiting **Dionisia Frankland** and **Edeva Campion.**

Order of Excalibur is a program instituted by the Duke of Cnobheresburg to bolster his Knighthood following and training, thus bridging the gap between Arthurian fiction and the Code of Conduct for a Chivalrous lifestyle.

Regina Cristina, Duchess of Elham, sister of the Duchess of Cnobheresburg, with Ladies-n-Waiting **Celestria Dumont and Anais Bauldry.**

Tang Sweord, a 37-inch, double-edged weapon for hacking and slashing through armor from an Anglo-Saxon design of that day. **Light-Bearer**, a Tang Sweord, presented as a special gift by the Duke to his son the Marquis after the Mercian battle. **Lightning**, a Tang Sweord with a bejeweled hilt owned by the Marquis. **Storm-Bringer,** a Tang Sweord, owned by the Elder Duke of Cnobheresburg.

Printed in the United States
by Baker & Taylor Publisher Services